Bruce Waldman

# Eimer Talpidae Mole's
## Fabulous Underground
## Food Adventure

By Michael A. Baker

Illustrated by Bruce Waldman

Eimer Talpidae Mole's Fabulous Underground Food Adventure
By Michael A. Baker
Illustrated by Bruce Waldman
Book design by Sharon Shiraga

Lake View Publishing
Post Office Box 8866
Scarborough, N.Y. 10510

ISBN 978-1-60643-234-1

To Susan, Jennifer and all teachers
who introduce words, growth and all
of earth's bounty to our children.

My name is Eimer Talpidae Mole 5TH, but you can call me Eimer. I'm a mole, and I've spent almost all my life in underground tunnels. Oh how I love those dark cool tunnels filled with dirt that holds delicious, scrumptious, delectable worms and bugs, which I love to eat! They taste so good!

Oh, sorry. I was getting carried away with thinking about those wonderful delicious worms and bugs. Oops, there I go again, but this is a story about food-people food. It's a story about my Great, Great, Great, Great Grandfather Eimer Talpidae Mole 1st, who had an underground food adventure that all people should know about.

*Cousin Desman*

But before I start my story, you should know something about moles. We look a little like mice, but we're NOT mice! We have big front feet with long fingernails—great for digging! We have long noses that are very sensitive. (By the way, I have a distant cousin who also has a sensitive nose that looks like a pin cushion.) We have small back feet that work great for pushing the dirt we dig out of the way to get to those bugs and worms.

We're almost blind, but don't feel sorry for us because in dark tunnels, we don't need to see well. We don't have any ears, which is good, because when we dig, dirt would just get in them. We're about 6 inches long, about as long as a short banana. We work hard and need energy, so we can eat twice our weight each day. I bet you can't do that!

We do come above ground sometimes but only to push up dirt. Go home and look at your lawn and if you see a little pile of dirt that looks like a little volcano, it's a mole hole built by one of us.

O.K. You know enough about moles. Now about Grandfather Eimer who lived two hundred years ago and dug tunnels and ate worms just like me. One day, while working hard in his tunnel, Grandfather Eimer was interrupted by the sound of people laughing and giggling and having a great old time on a hot summer day.

He was curious and came up through one of his mole holes in the
middle of a garden and spied a family of happy gardeners singing
praises to their beautiful tomatoes, lettuce, broccoli, and zucchini.

Then he heard a gardener yell "A mole, get the mole!" (I forgot to tell you that gardeners don't like moles because they say we dig tunnels under their plants and the plants fall into the holes and get ruined.) "Get the mole with the garden rake," they all screamed, and "WHAM"! A rake almost cut Grandfather Eimer's nose off. Grandfather was so frightened that he dove into his tunnel and ran fast.

But the danger was not past because you can see the top of a mole
tunnel above ground. Grandfather was fast, but "ZING"! A gardener
plunged a pointed stick into the tunnel and cut his tail, making him yell
"Oh that hurt!"

Grandfather ran into a deeper part of his tunnel so the gardeners wouldn't see him. He was deep in his tunnel when he heard one of the gardeners yell "Get a bucket of water. We'll drown him!" Then a minute later Grandfather heard a whooshing sound and water came gushing down his tunnel and suddenly he was under water swimming for his life. Holding his breath and swimming like a fish, he reached a high part of one of his distant tunnels and there was air, and he survived the attack of the gardeners.

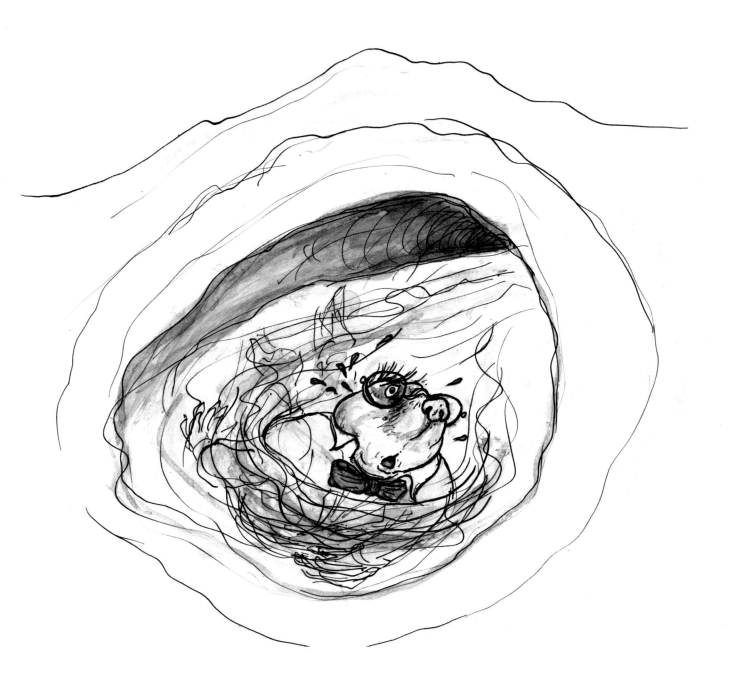

After that, Grandfather stayed as far away from the garden as he could for weeks, but one day he came close, and he could hear the family of gardeners crying "Oh what a tragedy! We are ruined and we are going to starve. What are we going to eat?"

Well, Grandfather was a very curious mole and he had to find out what had happened in the garden. So he slowly went back up his mole hole. But something was wrong; there was cold white powder in his hole. Using his big shovel feet, he pushed the white powder away and peeked over the edge of his mound, which was above ground, and was hit by freezing cold air. His head and nose were just high enough over the mound to see an awful sight. Ice and snow was all over the gardeners' tomatoes, zucchini, broccoli, and lettuce. And in the center of this scene, the gardeners were crying "It snowed in August. Impossible! Our tomatoes, zucchini, broccoli, and lettuce are ruined, and we will have no food to eat."

Grandfather Eimer was a kind mole, and even though the gardeners had tried to kill him, he still shed a tear because the gardeners would not have anything to eat and might starve. It was cold and Grandfather went back into his tunnel very upset and said to himself "These gardeners were mean to me, but they should not starve. And what about the baby gardeners, what will happen to them?"

Grandfather Eimer went deep into his warm tunnel and thought, "What can I do, how can I help? There is no way I can help. I'm just an underground mole. What do I know about the world above me and the food the gardeners need to survive? I just know dark tunnels and the things that grow underground."

Then Grandfather Eimer stopped and repeated the words " 'things that grow underground.' I wonder if the gardeners could eat some of those things that get in my way when I am digging in my tunnels? There are lots of hard, funny-shaped things I run into that look awful, and I have to dig around them. But maybe the gardeners could eat them!"

Grandfather dug many tunnels in search of his delicious, scrumptious, delectable worms and bugs. (There I go again. I'm getting hungry just telling this story.) He drew maps on the side of his home tunnel, maps of where he had dug and had come across hard, funny-shaped roadblocks.

Grandfather looked at the map on the wall and saw two he had tunneled around a few weeks ago and dashed off to investigate them. He stopped in front of the end of this large brown thing that didn't look appetizing at all and he said to himself, "How do I know the gardeners can eat this? I will have to take a bite. It's the only way." Grandfather then closed his little eyes and took a big bite. "Oh that tastes awful. It's hard, not juicy like a worm, but if the gardeners eat tomatoes, lettuce, and zucchini, maybe they would like this."

Grandfather Eimer started digging all around this funny hard roadblock and then pushed it all the way back to beneath his mole hole. He was sore all over his body from all his digging and pushing and said to himself "My poor tail and toes hurt so much."

As tired as he was, he trudged back to his home tunnel and looked on the map and spotted another funny roadblock he had drawn. With his poor eyesight, he made his way to a red object, bravely took a bite, and again yelled to himself, "Oh that tastes very bad, but those gardeners might eat it."

Grandfather worked hard to free the funny red thing, and after pushing it back to his mole hole, he collapsed with fatigue saying out loud, "I am beat. I have to go home and rest."

Grandfather Eimer went back to his home tunnel and fell into his bed and slept for 10 hours. When he woke up he thought, "Now I have to get the two things to the gardeners." He ran back to his mole hole and could hear the family above moaning, "It's hot again, but all our vegetables are ruined. They froze, and what will we eat when winter comes and we have no food?"

Grandfather thought, "Now is the time, but I hope they don't throw the rake at me again, and what am I going to say, 'Here, eat these funny hard things?' That makes no sense. I will have to give each of them a name."

He thought about the first one and how much his poor tail and toes hurt. "That's it. I will call it por-tale-toe, a po-ta-to. Now what about the other one? I was so beat after digging and pushing it. That's it. I will call it a beet."

Grandfather was scared but he had to do it, and with a burst of energy, he first pushed the potato through the opening of the mole hole and POP! It spun up and out. He then quickly pushed the beet through the hole and it landed at the foot of one of the gardeners. Grandfather then heard surprised shouts.

"What are these?"

Again with great bravery, Grandfather peeked over the top of the mole hole and shouted, "It is a potato and a beet, you can eat them and you won't starve."

The gardeners were so shocked they could not even remember that they had tried to kill Grandfather. All they could say was, "How do you know?"

"Because I ate a piece of each one. They are not tasty mole food, but the beet and potato can be food for the winter and keep you from starving until next year when you can plant a new garden."

Suddenly the gardeners realized that Grandfather Eimer Talpidae
Mole 1ST was a special mole who wanted to help them only because
they needed help. The big and the baby gardeners all yelled out
"Thank you mole for helping us. What is your name?"

"My name is Eimer Talpidae."

The gardeners replied "Eimer, we need more of your fabulous underground food. Lead us to more."

With those words, Eimer jumped down his mole hole and yelled, "Follow me in my tunnels and when I find more I will yell, 'Dig here for fabulous underground food'."

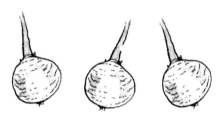

So that is my Grandfather's story about how he helped gardeners find underground food that can be stored for the long cold winters that always follow the hot summers.

Thanks for listening, but now I have to go and find some delicious, delectable, scrumptious worms and bugs.